Frederick

This Book Belongs To:

_____

Frederick

 Alfred A. Knopf, New York

THIS IS A BORZOI BOOK PUBLISHED BY ALFRED A. KNOPF
Copyright © 1967 by Leo Lionni
Copyright renewed 1995 by Leo Lionni

All rights reserved. Published in the United States by Alfred A. Knopf, an imprint of Random House Children's Books,
a division of Penguin Random House LLC, New York.

Knopf, Borzoi Books, and the colophon are registered trademarks of Penguin Random House LLC.

Visit us on the Web! randomhousekids.com
Kohls.com/Kids
Educators and librarians, for a variety of teaching tools, visit us at RHTeachersLibrarians.com

This special edition was printed for Kohl's Department Stores, Inc. (for distribution on behalf of Kohl's Cares, LLC,
its wholly owned subsidiary), by Random House Children's Books, a division of Penguin Random House LLC, New York.

Kohl's
1415111-00
123387
08/15 – 10/15

ISBN 978-0-375-97503-5
MANUFACTURED IN CHINA
10 9 8 7 6 5 4 3 2 1
Random House Children's Books supports the First Amendment and celebrates the right to read.

Frederick

All along the meadow where the cows grazed and the horses ran, there was an old stone wall.

In that wall, not far from the barn and the granary,
a chatty family of field mice had their home.

But the farmers had moved away, the barn was abandoned, and the granary stood empty. And since winter was not far off, the little mice began to gather corn and nuts and wheat and straw. They all worked day and night. All — except Frederick.

"Frederick, why don't you work?" they asked.
"I *do* work," said Frederick.
"I gather sun rays for the cold dark winter days."

And when they saw Frederick sitting there, staring at the meadow, they said, "And now, Frederick?" "I gather colors," answered Frederick simply. "For winter is gray."

And once Frederick seemed half asleep. "Are you dreaming, Frederick?" they asked reproachfully. But Frederick said, "Oh no, I am gathering words. For the winter days are long and many, and we'll run out of things to say."

The winter days came, and when the first snow fell
the five little field mice took to their hideout in the stones.

In the beginning there was lots to eat,
and the mice told stories of foolish foxes
and silly cats. They were a happy family.

But little by little they had nibbled up
most of the nuts and berries, the straw was
gone, and the corn was only a memory.
It was cold in the wall
and no one felt like chatting.

Then they remembered
what Frederick had said about sun rays
and colors and words.
"What about *your* supplies, Frederick?"
they asked.

"Close your eyes," said Frederick,
as he climbed on a big stone.
"Now I send you the rays of the sun.
Do you feel how their golden glow..."
And as Frederick spoke of the sun
the four little mice
began to feel warmer.
Was it Frederick's voice?
Was it magic?

"And how about the colors, Frederick?"
they asked anxiously. "Close your eyes again,"
Frederick said. And when he told them
of the blue periwinkles,
the red poppies in the yellow wheat,
and the green leaves
of the berry bush,
they saw the colors as clearly
as if they had been painted
in their minds.

"And the words, Frederick?"

Frederick cleared his throat,
waited a moment, and then,
as if from a stage, he said:

When Frederick had finished

'Who scatters snowflakes? Who melts the ice?
Who spoils the weather? Who makes it nice?
Who grows the four-leaf clovers in June?
Who dims the daylight? Who lights the moon?

Four little field mice who live in the sky.
Four little field mice . . . like you and I.

One is the Springmouse who turns on the showers.
Then comes the Summer who paints in the flowers.
The Fallmouse is next with walnuts and wheat.
And Winter is last . . . with little cold feet.

Aren't we lucky the seasons are four?
Think of a year with one less . . . or one more!"

they all applauded. "But Frederick," they said, "you are a poet!"

Frederick blushed, took a bow, and said shyly, "I know it."